The Happiness Tree

CELEBRATING THE GIFTS
OF TREES WE TREASURE

Andrea Alban Gosline

BY Andrea Alban Gosline

ILLUSTRATED BY Lisa Burnett Bossi

*For Emma—
May you find a
favorite tree to
read your
books
beside!*

♡

Treena! ♡

FEIWEL AND FRIENDS

NEW YORK

"Everything good begins with me,"
the acorn told its mother tree,
and drifted on the dancing breeze
to find a cloak of golden leaves.

Protected from the windy snap,
the acorn shared a winter's nap
with dreams of saplings growing wild,
a treasure tree for every child.

Above the seeds, old nature stilled
but deep beneath, the earthworms tilled
and dug long tunnels through the soil
with crops of roots in constant toil.

When spring arrived, the seeds awoke
and gave the gritty ground a poke,
then sprouted in the fragrant air
among the elders standing bare.

From tender stem to sturdy trunk,
each tree revealed its leafy spunk
and welcomed friends to nest the crown
as summer's sun and moon shone down.

Warm wishes sowed the greening land
and flocking birds rejoiced the stand
and sang a story that uplifts,
the tale of ten trees' simple gifts.

I am the tree of
hope

I welcome morning's ringing light,

dream with crescent moons at night,

expect the joy that rainbows bring,

anticipate unfurling spring.

I begin

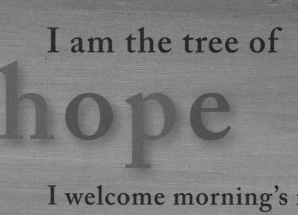

I am the tree of
love

I hold a pair of doves aloft,
nurture nestlings feathered soft,
shelter creatures small and new,
treasure friendship tried and true.

I adore

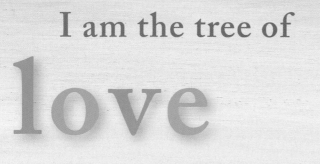

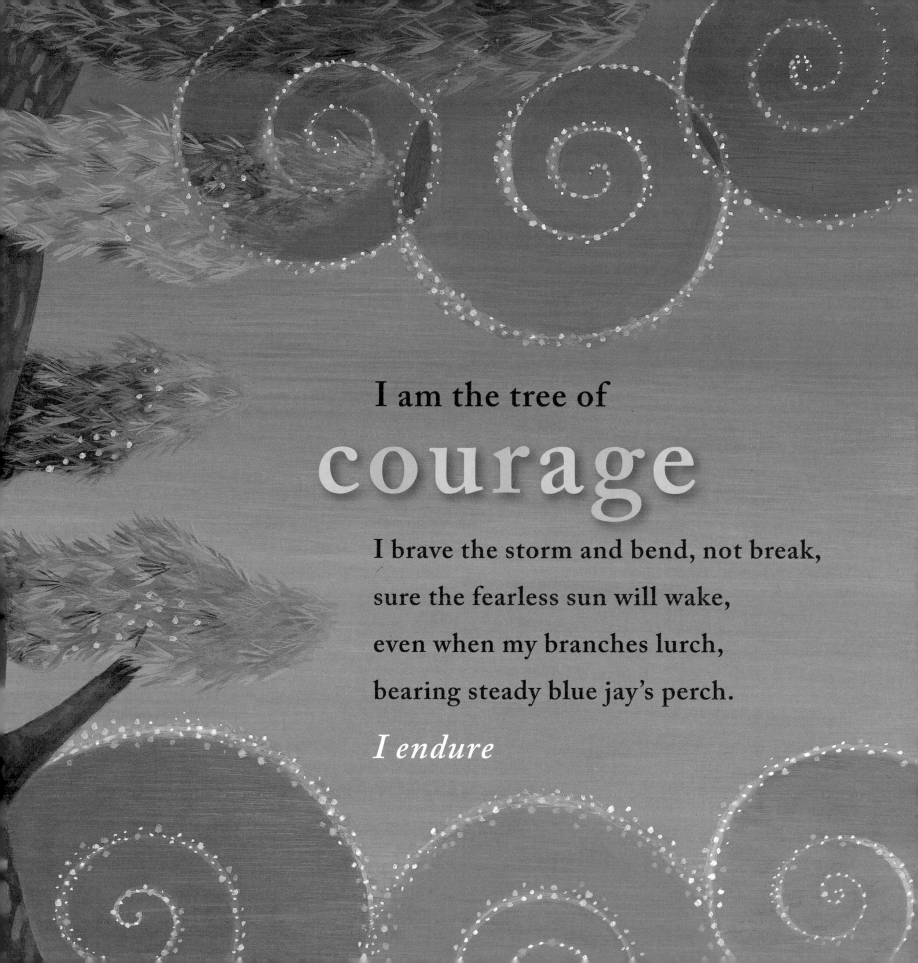

I am the tree of

courage

I brave the storm and bend, not break,

sure the fearless sun will wake,

even when my branches lurch,

bearing steady blue jay's perch.

I endure

I am the tree of
gratitude

I give my thanks for rainy days,
cotton clouds crowned with rays,
refreshing air the forest clears,
quench my thirst as summer nears.

I appreciate

I am the tree of
peace

I balance my beloved friend
in quiet spots where spirits mend,
below the bunting's patient home,
come contemplate the paths you roam.

I renew

I am the tree of

compassion

I understand the planet's woes,
pray from dawn 'til daisies close
for kindness, blessings, and rebirth,
of all that's good for mother earth.

I shelter

I am the tree of
tolerance

I reach out in freedom's name,

respecting no two are the same,

the different ways we grow and live,

mistakes we make and still forgive.

I accept

I am the tree of

generosity

I send the critters winter's green,

springtime dazzle in between,

shade for summer's picnic lunch,

autumn pods for feet to crunch.

I provide

I am the tree of

honesty

I surrender strong and true,
build a bridge from me to you,
revealing great integrity
in honor of a trusted tree.

I open

I am the tree of
happiness

I create a world of joy
around the laughing girl and boy,
underneath the boughs of trees,
celebrate my majesty.

I delight

"Everything good begins right here,"
the children in the circle cheer,

and with this wish, a forest in scope,
is growing from one seed of hope.

I stand for hope.

I am the White Oak tree. My scientific name is *Quercus alba* and I belong to the Beech family. My flowers turn into nubbins, which become acorns in autumn when I shed all of my leaves. Squirrels, blue jays, and woodpeckers hide my acorns in their homes or bury them in the ground. But most of my acorns are hidden by my own falling leaves. For every 10,000 acorns, only one will become an oak tree. I am the official tree of the United States.

I stand for love.

I am the Yellow Poplar tree but people often call me the "tulip tree" because of my tulip-shaped leaves. My scientific name is *Liriodendron tulipifera* and I belong to the Magnoliaceae family. Honeybees pollinate my flowers. My cone-shaped fruit stores samaras (seeds with wings), until they fly away in the autumn and winter. I attract hummingbirds and squirrels and I am a host for butterflies.

I am the White Pine tree. My scientific name is *Pinus strobus* and I belong to the Pinaceae family. My trunk is very straight and can reach over 100 feet in height. I am the tallest tree in North America's eastern region and the only native five-needle pine. My cones are thornless and have

I stand for courage.

scales. My two-winged seeds can travel 700 feet out in the open. Black bear cubs climb me to safety and bald eagles build their nests below my crown top. My tallest relative is called "Boogerman Pine" and stands 185 feet tall in the Great Smoky Mountains National Park.

I stand for gratitude.

I am the Sugar Maple tree. My scientific name is *Acer saccharum* and I belong to the Aceraceae family. In the fall, my leaves turn from bright yellow to orange to fluorescent red-orange. My fruit is horseshoe-shaped with two winged seeds. I draw water from deep in the soil to quench my thirst and then water the drier upper layers, where plants such as blackberry and red raspberry shrubs grow. I am tapped early in the spring for my sweet sap, which is boiled or evaporated to make maple syrup. My leaf is featured on the Canadian flag.

I am the Flowering Dogwood tree.

My scientific name is *Cornus florida* and I belong to the Cornaceae family. In the spring, I am covered with pink or white flowers. In autumn, my leaves turn bright red and I grow shiny red fruit called

I stand for peace.

drupe. But don't eat them because they are poisonous to people. I like to grow beneath taller trees. Many forest animals take cover under my candelbra-like branches. I attract wild birds like the Tufted Titmouse and Northern Bobwhite. I depend on bees, beetles, butterflies, and other insects to help pollinate me.

I am the American Elm tree.

My scientific name is *Ulmus americana* and I belong to the Ulmaceae family. My trunk can become four feet wide and is usually

I stand for compassion.

divided into several large limbs. My leaves are edged with "teeth," and my winged seeds are round and have a paper-like texture. Many birds build their nests in my drooping branches. In the early 20th century, a shipment of lumber from Europe carrying infected bark beetles killed many of my relatives. But I am making a comeback now thanks to groups of elmlovers.

I stand for tolerance.

I am the Blue Spruce tree.

My scientific name is *Picea pungens Engelm* and I belong to the Pinaceae family. My four-sided needles are a beautiful silver-blue color and have a very sharp point on the end. I provide cover and seeds for squirrels, rodents, and birds. I can live to be 600-800 years old. My largest relative, a state and national champion big tree, lives in Gunnison National Forest. He stands 126 feet tall and has a trunk that is five foot in diameter. The National Christmas Tree in Washington, D.C., is a 40-foot tall Blue Spruce.

I am the Southern Magnolia tree.

My scientific name is *Magnolia grandiflora* and I belong to the Magnoliaceae family. I have large, saucer-shaped white flowers that can scent an entire garden. My oval-shaped leaves are evergreen. My crown reminds people of wide-

I stand for generosity.

open arms. In the fall, my fuzzy brown cones ripen with bright red seeds, attracting birds. I am an ancient tree species. I evolved before bees. Fossilized specimens of my ancestors have been discovered dating back 20 million years.

I am the Paper Birch tree.

My scientific name is *Betula papyrifera* and I belong to the Betulaceae family. I have one or multiple thin trunks and a narrow crown. My bark is white and flakes off

I stand for honesty.

easily in papery strips or sheets. My flowers are called catkins and my fruit are called winged nutlets. I am a favorite feeding tree of red squirrels, hummingbirds, and yellow-bellied sapsuckers who peck holes in my bark to feed on my sap. People make syrup, wine, beer, and medicinal tonics from my sap.

I stand for happiness.

I am the Redwood tree.

My scientific name is *Sequoia sempervirens* which means "forever living" or "forever green." I belong to the Cupressaceae family. My forests are known as nature's cathedrals. I lift water to the height of my crown, which may be as tall as a thirty-five-story skyscraper. An entire ecosystem lives in the canopy of my forest, high above the cool mists of the forest floor. My young seedlings grow in a circle with their elders. I live practically forever, up to 2,000 years old. My roots never die.

America's State Trees

The year in parentheses refers to the date each tree was designated as a state tree.

Alabama: Southern Longleaf Pine (1997)

Alaska: Sitka Spruce (1962)

Arizona: Palo Verde (1954)

Arkansas: Pine (1939)

California: California Redwood (1937)

Colorado: Colorado Blue Spruce (1939)

Connecticut: White Oak (1947)

Delaware: American Holly (1939)

Florida: Sabal Palmetto Palm (1953)

Georgia: Live Oak (1937)

Hawaii: Kukui Tree (1959)

Idaho: White Pine (1935)

Illinois: White Oak (1973)

Indiana: Tulip Tree (1931)

Iowa: Oak (1961)

Kansas: Eastern Cottonwood (1937)

Kentucky: Tulip Poplar (1994)

Louisiana: Baldcypress (1963)

Maine: White Pine (1945)

Maryland: White Oak (1941)

Massachusetts: American Elm (1941)

Michigan: White Pine (1955)

Minnesota: Red Pine (1945)

Mississippi: Magnolia (1938)

Missouri: Flowering Dogwood (1955)

Montana: Ponderosa Pine (1949)

Nebraska: Cottonwood (1972)

Nevada: Pinon Pine (1953)

New Hampshire: White Birch (1947)

New Jersey: Red Oak (1950)

New Mexico: Nut Pine or Pinon Tree (1949)

New York: Sugar Maple (1956)

North Carolina: Pine (1963)

North Dakota: American Elm (1947)

Ohio: Ohio Buckeye (1953)

Oklahoma: Redbud (1937)

Oregon: Douglas-fir (1939)

Pennsylvania: Eastern Hemlock (1931)

Rhode Island: Red Maple (1964)

South Carolina: Cabbage Palmetto (1939)

South Dakota: Black Hills Spruce (1947)

Tennessee: Tulip Poplar (1947)

Texas: Pecan (1919)

Utah: Blue Spruce (1933)

Vermont: Sugar Maple (1949)

Virginia: Dogwood (1956)

Washington: Western Hemlock (1947)

West Virginia: Sugar Maple (1949)

Wisconsin: Sugar Maple (1949)

Wyoming: Cottonwood (1947)

....

*Canada's national arboreal emblem
is the Maple Tree. (1996)*

PLANT A HAPPINESS TREE
ON ARBOR DAY

It is well that you should celebrate your Arbor Day

thoughtfully, for within your lifetime

the nation's need of trees will become serious.

~THEODORE ROOSEVELT, 1907 ARBOR DAY

A wide selection of tree seedlings are available at your local nursery or through

the National Arbor Day Foundation at www.arborday.org or 888-448-7337.

FOR OUR DADS

Jan Alban, who believed

"one is nearer God's heart in a garden."

~ A. A. G.

Bill Burnett ~ happiest

out amongst his trees. ~ L. B. B.

A Feiwel and Friends Book
An Imprint of Macmillan

Library of Congress Cataloging-in-Publication Data Available

ISBN-13: 978-0-312-37017-6
ISBN-10: 0-312-37017-2

The artwork was created with fluid acrylics on watercolor paper
Book design by Lisa Bossi and Barbara Grzeslo
Feiwel and Friends logo designed by Filomena Tuosto

First Edition: September 2008

1 3 5 7 9 10 8 6 4 2

www.feiwelandfriends.com